What is Wrong with These Mothers-in-Law?

by

Raphael Grenel

RoseDog Books
PITTSBURGH, PENNSYLVANIA 15238

RoseDog Books
585 Alpha Drive, Suite 103
Pittsburgh, PA 15238
Visit our website at *www.rosedogbookstore.com*

ISBN: 979-8-89127-761-8
eISBN: 979-8-89127-259-0

What is Wrong with These Mothers-in-Law?

by

Raphael Grenel

Table of Contents

Prologue

"NO!!! I disapprove of this unity!" yells out the Queen mother.

"But, I am in love with her!" yells out the young man in the room.

The Queen mother says, "I SAID NO! She is not good enough for you. She looks more like a wench, a gold-digger, someone not worthy of my prince."

Every culture, every religion, and even nobility, no matter where you live, there is some kind of hierarchy for the approval of their marriage. The "Queen" (mother/mother-in-law) would be the one to authorize the approval of the marriage for her "prince" or "princess". The "King" (father/father-in-law) will either stand side-by-side with the "Queen's Order" or he will back up the decision. If the King is backing up the "Queen's Order", he is basically saying, "I AM NOT TRYING TO PISS THIS WOMAN OFF, OKAY!?"

When you think of mothers-in-law (MILs), you would think that you will have another mother. Even though she will not be blood related, she should be like your own mother. Having that mindset, you will automatically have a template of a mother in your mind (comparing your mother to theirs). They will have some traits that will be the same, and some will be something totally different. There are even a few that are just hard to explain. Throughout the world, mothers tend to have their own way of raising their children to get through school, also puberty along the way. Some are the natural way, some are a little strict, and some are the customary way. I would not mind it being a little strict to make sure everyone follows the rules. But customary sounds chaotic and barbaric, ugh.

Mothers should be appreciated for all the work and difficulties she goes through throughout her life. She should be placed on a throne and be worshiped but not too much. That "entitled" gene will come out, and she will start to want to be praised all the time. Just remember, a little praise here and there would be enough.

Through this book, from all my own research of the stories of mothers and mothers-in-law, I collaborated this information for the public to recognize the signs of the mannerisms to alert you for in the near future.

Chapter 1

The Mothers of Yesterday To Today

Let's go talk to Professor Peabody and hop into the "Way-Back Machine" to learn how the mothers of yesterday helped keep things in line at home. Now, back in the day, everyone in the family household had their own responsibilities:

Father: went to work and made the money for the home. Also handled the maintenance of the house.

Mother: maintained the house duties and also taught those duties to her daughter.

Son/daughter: went to school, as well as extracurricular activities.

This had been the staple template throughout the early years.

Both mother and father tried to teach the children the basic life lessons: chores, dating, further education, a career, marriage, and children. As the children grew older and they had their own children, they tended to mirror those life lessons that were taught from their parents. This had been true throughout history in every country and every culture.

The problem was that when the children started discovering what was out there in the real world, they tended to not stick with those lessons. Since the world had been changing and evolving, so had the children. All of a sudden, the children had started to do as they pleased: hanging out at all times, getting into trouble, having kids at a very early age, dropping out of school, etc.

At this time, the parents felt they loosened their reins too much. Now, it was time to go from home mother to "Supermom" mode. She would go wherever the children were to control the chaos that lay in the wake:

Skipping school: is it the teacher's fault or the students? She would go up to the school and raise holy hell to find out.

Pregnancy: get an abortion or find out who the father is and hold him accountable.

Hanging out late on a school night: find them and embarrass them in front of their friends, lol.

Getting in trouble with the law: let them spend a couple of nights in jail to teach them a lesson (hopefully a hard one).

Mothers tend to have a kind of sixth-sense for when they feel a member of the family. If they sense anything weird, she will call everyone so she can get into contact with anyone to find out what is going on. Which is great. However, she will go above and beyond to make sure everything is done right. Sometimes, they will go the "entitled" or "Karen" route and get someone ASAP to make sure they are taken care of immediately. They will go as far as going to jail for their cause. My question is, "CAN YOU PLEASE WAIT FOR AT LEAST TWO MINUTES, PLEASE?!" For some, they will be patient enough as long as you are polite and courteous to them. Others, well...they will literally fight you AND the police, especially if they do not get their way.

What is it about mothers that at one moment they are the sweetest that you have ever seen, and the next moment, they are "Satan". You had to do something really bad or really stupid to get her there. Some say it is natural, others say it is menopause. Trying to calm the storm that is "Satan" is very tricky. Honestly, the best way to do this is to "kill them with kindness" approach. Yes, I know "is that way played out though?" Trust me, it is not. A peace offering is good, but just enough to tame the monster-in-law.

I wonder, if mothers of yesterday were here today, I believe that at least 75 percent of the chaos would be controlled in time. Baby steps, baby steps. Of course, 25 percent will still do as they please. Well, maybe we can invent a machine that can change the personality of our wild children to be responsible ones. Then we can all be happy. That would be great. It might be better to use it on monsters-in-law, lol. Especially when they go "Full Satan", lol.

Social get-togethers were common back then. The ladies got together for potlucks and card games. Of course, there were also talks about the latest shoes and/or clothing they just bought. The other half of the talk was about their children and their schooling. You would always hear a lot of "my child has been accepted into a prestigious school", whether it would be elementary, junior high, high school, or college. The key word is always "prestige"; the more famous the school, the higher the status. This is where the "entitlement" is born from. They will then feel so superior, everyone else below them will look inferior. In time, they will want to socialize with other like-minded women of the same social status. It is the same way as their husbands being part of a big corporation. The bigger the name of the company, and the higher the position, the more "prestige" the wife has.

Don't get me started with the galas and fundraisers that would give them a great opportunity to flaunt their wealth. The extravagant gowns, the expensive jewelry, the latest hairstyles, the massive egos, lol. I'm pretty sure there would have been so many turned up noses in the air, that all of them were smelling something really bad (kind of hoping that you do not see a bunch of nose hairs that should have been taken care of before leaving the house, lol).

Whew!!! I swear, you will either need when dealing with the "entitled ones", lol: a full-body armor suit, a bulletproof vest, full riot gear...better yet, just call a SWAT team to try to control the chaos. Or, at least, move to another country or island to get away from the madness.

I do believe mothers of today who feel "entitled", teach their children how to be "entitled", and release them into the world to wreak havoc and take everything. The biggest problem is running into them and/or marrying one. Perish the thought.

Chapter 2

Introductions and the "Switch"

Throughout the years, it is proper to introduce your fiancé to the families for their approval of acceptance. The majority of the time, these meetings would go off well without a hitch. The few times they end up not approving are by bringing a TON of questions, just like coming into a firing squad (you can picture it, can you, lol). Those questions are the bullets, and you are nothing but a target to them. Honestly, no one is really prepared for the onslaught of crazy questions that will most likely come from mothers-in-law.

Now, let me introduce you to the "switch".

At the time of introductions of their fiancé, this switch trips. This invisible switch is connected to a meter that starts in the middle for judging the fiancé from the very beginning.

The meter is connected to the brain and throughout the body to react to their child's fiancé. They would start looking and reacting to the questions being answered: age, family, school/degrees, hobbies, marriage, and children (how many), and so on and so forth. The answers the fiancé gives would give the mother-in-law that meter to sway back and forth for her mood. Any good answers would sway the meter to the left. Any bad answers would sway the meter to the right. A lot of good answers, you may start seeing an angel's halo (maybe wings). A lot of bad answers, you may start seeing devil horns (maybe a tail). Here are some things I would suggest going through when it comes to mothers-in-law first meetings:

Age: The majority of mothers would like their child's partner to be up to or under two years from their child's age. Almost anything beyond those two years, the mother will start looking at her funny, and start saying things like, "Why did you pick this old lady?" or "This high schooler?"

Family: Honestly, this is very important to the mother. Especially the size of the family. Now, if by chance the fiancé had been raised by a single parent, you should immediately glaze over before the mother starts diving deeper into why. Mothers are masters of getting information. The only other way you can avoid the subject is when the child warns his/her mother way ahead of time. If by chance she tries to go there, stop her immediately or leave immediately.

School/degree: Being book-smart is definitely a plus (especially on really good argument comebacks, lol). Having a degree will at least grease the wheel of approval. I believe any degree will be reasonable. As long as it is a worthwhile degree that will give you a good and exciting career. A word of caution: please, please, PLEASE DO NOT say you have a "Liberal Arts" degree. Your future mother-in-law's face will look like "Are you kidding me?" There is really nothing wrong with getting a degree. But for an educated MIL, she would believe that her child's fiancé should have a more meaningful degree for a better future.

Hobbies: Hobbies are great to have fun and relieve stress from work and everyday life (includes MILs). The basics include cooking, visiting museums, boating, painting, knitting, traveling, etc. Some hobbies you will have to watch out for because MIL will ask to accompany you, ugh (you are trying to relieve your stress, not add to it).

Engagement and marriage: This will get asked even if you guys are only dating right now. Mothers-in-law will try to pressure for possible confirmation dates of popping the question. Just mention you are still trying to know each other and each others' families. Everything takes time. Once you feel your partner IS the one you cannot live without, then go for it. A word of caution: when you do make the announcement, the mother-in-law will want to be involved in every step of the planning. Definitely try to limit her to a minimum amount of things to do (the bare minimum). She may want to try to make it like SHE was getting married (shudder).

Children: Yes, she will definitely ask if they are having children and how many. Some mothers-in-law would like as many as they can produce. Also, she would prefer boys instead of girls. A little secret: grandchildren are like kryptonite to in-laws. They can really soothe the MILs (monsters-in-law).

There are other questions she may ask you, hopefully not too personal. If by some chance the in-laws would try, you should excuse yourself to the restroom or outside to avoid them to cool off. If the MIL/family continues to pressure you, apologize and say you do not feel well and want to go home. A few things to remember when meeting your partner's family for the first time:

Look presentable. Casual wear will do, nothing flashy.

Be yourself. DO NOT come off as someone else. They will pick up on that quick.

As mentioned before, a little bit of information to appease the masses.

Ask your partner about their mother's favorite things as far as drinks/snacks as a welcoming gift.

Chapter 3

Engagement & Worry
Picture this:

At a famous casual restaurant, a private room is set with the soft light of candles. Romantic music plays softly in the background. As dinner concludes, the waiter clears the plates and mentions that dessert will be out in a few minutes.

A few minutes later, as if right on time, the dessert was presented. It comes covered up, presented like a presentation. The gentleman says "thank you" to the waiter, and then he leaves the table. The gentleman says to the lady accompanying him, "I have a special surprise for you. Please take off the cover." The lady slowly uncovers the dessert tray to show a two-layer cake of her favorite flavor, with some writing on the top of it. It reads, "WILL YOU MARRY ME?" While she is reading the cake, the gentleman rises from his seat and bends down on one knee, presenting a beautiful engagement ring. She sees the ring and covers her mouth with both hands as she is speechless. She nods and whispers, "Yes". He puts the ring on her finger, and they kiss and hug each other for what seems like hours.

Okay, enough with the waterworks, lol. The process pretty much starts with the meeting for the first time. With that in mind, let's go all the way back to the 1800s, when an interested couple would ask for permission to date or "court" each other from each side. There was (and still is) also the traditional way with arranged marriages. This is the meeting of the couple, as well as the parents, for the first time. Usually the meeting is set up by a professional matchmaker (around half of the time, it will be the mother).

Another thing about arranged marriages is that they are like a "business deal". Going back in time, these types of marriages try to form a "deal of convenience" for both parties. From middle-class to nobility, they know that by combining resources, they will get richer and more powerful. It still falls back to the relationship with the couple. With mothers in particular, they always want the union to work out. With this union, it means more power, more money, more prestige. And some will do whatever it takes to make it happen. Including sabotage (yes, they will go there).

Through the history of time, women have found different ways to make situations go their way to stay on top. That said, it is still as prominent today.

Now, from the moment of the announcement of the engagement, that meter (from Chapter 2), is starting to move toward the "evil" side. The reason for this action is that she is starting to feel threatened that their child's attention will be less on her and more on the partner. At this point, she will try to make their child's attention more on her, trying anything and everything to get it back. From calling their phone for anything from morning till past midnight, to having them run errands, to taking her with you on trips. Even to try hooking them up with someone else (WTF).

At the same time, she will find a way to lightly talk bad about the partner and then UNO reverse that and say that the partner is talking bad about her. Gradually, she will turn up the insults for the partner to either endure the insults or get fed up ending the relationship. Even gossip about the partner to her friends and neighbors.

If, and this is a BIG if, you can endure the mental and sarcastic comments from her, may I suggest keeping a good distance from her.

Also, keep communications to a bare minimum.

When you have to talk to her, try going through a person, or by text, or by email. For those few times you have to be in her presence, I would suggest investing into a micro-recorder and/or your phone for all conversations to prove to your fiancé that you are being harassed by her. Then you can take on the situation with the necessary steps to control the chaos that is the mother-in-law.

Chapter 4

The Wedding and the War

A loving couple on their wedding day cannot wait for those last magical words, "I NOW PRONOUNCE YOU MAN AND WIFE! YOU MAY KISS THE BRIDE". Then the man

lifts the veil and then the couple kiss and the preacher announces to everyone, "MAY I PRESENT TO YOU MR. AND MRS. SMITH!!!"

Everyone stands and claps for the new couple.

You do have to wonder, if you have never been married or been invited to a wedding, it is a very long road to get to the altar. That old saying comes to mind, "a journey of a 1000 miles begins with a single step." Especially when mothers-in-law try to get involved and make it about her rather than the couple, ugh. That is when the "Karen" comes out and presses for that "credit/acknowledgement" of trying to put the wedding together herself (yes, it is that bad). Remember: power, money, prestige.

It would not be surprising that the mother-in-law already has a whole wedding binder full of all of her favorite things. From the beginning of the planning process to the honeymoon (she definitely needs a better hobby). The best course of action is to have a get-together of a "wedding planning party" and assign duties to gather information on prices for the assigned tasks. You can fully shortcut it and hire a wedding planner. They are a little expensive but will get every detail done with no problem. However, planning it yourself with your family and close circle of friends would be more fun, personal, and meaningful. Make sure you assign your maid-of-honor to one of your close friends ASAP before mother-in-law tries to push the assignment to her daughter or cousin. The biggest reason is to fill the MIL with information about wedding details (A.K.A. flying monkeys). With the information that is related to MIL, she can try to change up anything to her liking, especially if she tries changing it at the last minute.

There are a TON of wedding stories that depict the mother-in-law as the main ringleader for interfering in the details that will make a joyous occasion into a nightmare. To control the chaos that is mother-in-law, you may either have to hire someone like a close circle friend or a private investigator to follow her every move to stay at least 2–3 steps ahead of her antics during the process. Speaking of the process, I looked at a template of a wedding duty list that you would go through. WOW!!! I finally see why there is so much to go through that people would lose their minds for, and where "Bridezillas" are born from. And the MOH is supposed to be the buffer, to try to calm her down as much as possible. Especially when MIL tries to suggest (try to force) changes that SHE wants. Just remember: you are fighting a "war" against a woman who wants things to her liking and not yours.

Now for the grand scheme of things. If I try to list everything from the wedding to-do list, I would have developed a serious case of carpal tunnel and need surgery. So, I will list the most important things mother-in-law will try really hard to control. In no particular order:

Food: Yes, I'm starting with one of the top problematic arguments. For the food, you would try to accommodate everyone who will be in attendance. Including, if anyone has any type of food allergies. Mother-in-law will want to go to the taste-test herself and make mental notes on which food SHE will want to replace and not care about anyone else. You will have to make sure that you check, double-check, and triple-check the menu and the specific ingredients. Make sure you have some kind of security measure to protect any type of changes, like a password and/or presenting an ID when you arrive.

The wedding cake: how many are attending (size of it), a taste test, color, and design. Sometimes the couple would want a small ceremony; others would want a big extravagant wedding. Mother-in-law will try to change the size for many more people that SHE will invite unexpectedly, the flavor of the cake from the original, and the color and design to her liking. Who knows, she may invite from 20 to 50 extra guests. WTF!!! Again, password and in-person changes, please!!!

Reception: For the wedding itself, depending on the couple's choice, will most likely be a small intimate wedding chapel. Some will go to church. And a few will simply elope (courthouse). Like before, mother-in-law will try to invite HER close personal friends, and it will end up being a greater number of uninvited guests and will make sure the venues will be big enough. If this is not caught in time, everything will be overrun, and the food will run out almost halfway through the reception. Most likely, this would start a huge commotion, up to starting a riot.

Music: Music is pretty much straight-forward. You can either hire a DJ or make your own playlist and use a nice size Bluetooth speaker to dance the night away. Make sure mother-in-law keeps her distance from it, so it would not change to suit her taste.

Decor: Repeat after me: YOUR COLORS, YOUR RULES!!! YOUR COLORS, YOUR RULES!!! Everyone has their own dream of the perfect setting, decorations, and colors for their dream wedding. Mother-in-law WILL definitely give her 2 cents (and an extra penny) with her so-called "experience". "Everything in here is too bright", "These colors do not blend well together", "These flower arrangements are all wrong", and everything else under the sun. Do try to control yourself from going at her with the cake knife, lol. Warn your MOH to hide all sharp and pointed objects, lol.

Bar: You know a good amount of people cannot hold their liquor at all. Especially when you know those do not need to drink. Do make sure the bar is well-stocked up with the usual liquor, wine, and soft drinks so everyone has a good time. I will advise you that you should warn the chaperone you hired to be on high alert to watch mother-in-law intake of wine and mixed drinks, so she will not only embarrass herself, but also the people in the venue. Especially when it comes to giving speeches, ugh (can you picture a very drunk MIL trying to give a speech in slur, lol).

The dress: Oh boy...this is always a huge issue because everyone has different tastes and styles of wedding dresses. Some like the traditional dress. Others like to go sophisticated. And a handful will go all-out and go with something crazy. When I looked at the different kinds of wedding dresses on the internet, my computer almost crashed with so, so many dresses, wow. "Hey, I was looking for a simple wedding dress. Not one with eight pieces to it!!!" Yeah, I thought the rest of my little list was enough. This is a very, very time-consuming deal with maybe some intricate details to make it as perfect as possible. And knowing your mother-in-law, she will try to go against a lot of what you want. "Too much lace", "not poofy enough", "the back is too exposed", "showing too much cleavage", etc. Remember: do not kill her, too many witnesses, lol. A good way to save on spending a lot on a wedding dress is to ask mother, mother-in-law, grandmother, and grandmother-in-law about their wedding dresses. You can then pick in-between them. Go to get it altered to fit you. Then, all you would need are the shoes, hair, and makeup.

After everything else, from the remaining list, the wedding is finally here. The festivities are in full swing, and everyone is having a great time. Still, keeping at least one eye on mother-in-law for her antics. And after everything is said and done, the loving couple is going on their honeymoon destination. And everyone has passed out from the party.

Chapter 5

Grandchildren and Peace (Somewhat)

Children are a blessing and a miracle in disguise. They will bring you a lot of joy and pain and a bunch of other different emotions in between. For new parents, they would want to keep their newborn in a protective, environmentally-controlled house so no harm can come to them. Some would like to keep them in a protective bubble, although they may get really cranky really easily. But you can only do the best you can by doing what the doctor says and not herbal or ancient medicine. Yes, that also includes essential oils, lol.

Grandparents are very happy to see their grandchildren because they know their legacy and bloodline will continue throughout the years. When they get together, they will entertain each other to their heart's content. Of course, the grandparents will spoil their grandchildren; just remind them to not spoil them too much.

I have noticed there are some similarities between both grandchildren and grandparents. Here are a few listed:

They bring joy to each other lives.

They both love snacks.

They are both full of energy.

They both are cranky if they don't take their required naps.

They both wear diapers in case of accidents.

Another great thing about grandparents is that they have the patience to teach the little ones about right and wrong. Rewarding them for doing good is a great teaching method and doing bad will likely punish them. When they are at that curious age, they would teach them their particular hobby (woodworking, knitting, gardening, farming, etc.). As the children grow, those hobbies that were taught will eventually become something they will teach to their children.

Grandparents can also be a curse for the grandchildren. The reason for this being that children's minds are like sponges; they will soak up the information of what they read and what is said about anyone. Especially when the grandparents start talking bad about their mother/father. And whatever the children hear, just like a parrot, they will most likely repeat what they said. "Grandma says she does not like you", "She says you cannot cook", "She says you keep the house dirty", "She says you always wear old clothes", etc. At that point, you have every right to not only ban the kids from coming over, but you have permission to go "Full Mamabear Mode" on her, lol.

There are also the grandparents trying to bribe the children with toys and great outings to make them more favorable to them. This is a noticeable red flag. Once you start noticing this, start keeping the children as far away from them as much as possible. Instead, take them to the other grandparent's home. If your spouse questions as to why the kids are at MY parent's home, have a sit-down talk with him and discuss what the kids have been hearing. Draw out a plan for any time you have to take the kids to your mother-in-law and supervise the visits only. Also, have a little meeting with MIL and sternly warn her that if there are any bad or harsh words about the spouse or any rumors going forward, there will be no contact from them for a period of time. Yeah, sometimes you have to play dirty with them to get things in order.

Chapter 6

Besides a Stake or a Silver Bullet, How Do You Handle Mothers-In-Law?

Mothers-in-law are like a bad rash: the more she irritates you, the more you want to scratch to relieve the irritation. The best way to cure it is to either medicate it (as in she takes some sleeping pills) or cut it off (now, where is that machete? lol) Cutting it out would definitely be the last resort. However, we all wish it was that easy.

Mothers-in-law always like to be in their child's life from birth, through puberty, through graduations, through marriage. But, when it comes to the couple wanting time to themselves, she will want to visit to see how they are doing. Or heaven forbid, move in with them, ugh. Especially if MIL does not like their child's partner.

Throughout the years and certain customs, a married couple would move into the parents-in-law home for "wife training".

Basically, MIL (and sometimes DIL) will "teach" their child's spouse how to clean correctly, do laundry correctly, use the right ingredients while cooking, and to learn how to address the guests and relatives who come to visit. There are also morning visits. She will come by and criticize anything and everything about the cleanliness of the house. She will also sit there, watch her, and belittle how she does the cleaning. And after a while, before her son comes home, she will leave and go to her home. It's like an adrenaline rush to make her feel good about herself instead of picking up a natural hobby like knitting, traveling, SOMETHING THAT REQUIRES HER TO KEEP BUSY, lol.

All of this just sounds more like the wife becoming a housekeeper. Believe it or not, this tradition is still ongoing today. However, from this generation alone, that tradition may just die out. The reason: this generation just wants to have fun and be free to do as they wish every

day. Sure, they will handle their responsibilities of paying for their cost of living by working a good paying job and having a family. Maybe later down the line, they will want to try the traditions again. But, for now, nope.

Back to the couple moving in with the in-laws. There really should be "no" type of house training because you learned all the basics when you were in your young teens. You know, cooking, cleaning, laundry, responsibilities, all the things learned growing up in your home with your parents. When you are an adult, these lessons are used for everyday living to have a clean household of your own. But mother-in-law will try to find ways to judge you on anything to mess with you.

WHAT IS WRONG WITH THESE MOTHERS-IN-LAW?

What will really cross the line: when she wants to call you at your job for really little mundane things. Like wanting to talk about anything, to asking for favors to grab something for her, to paying a bill for her (with your own money, no paybacks). If you cannot do something she asks of you, she will try to sabotage your career (yes, this is so true). The very first time that she attempts this act, immediately alert your boss, and get a lawyer to get her a cease and desist order.

Mothers-in-law love to stay in control of her own universe, including who her child's partner should be.

ATTENTION!!! ATTENTION!!! This is an alert to all young women out there who are looking for their soulmate: DO NOT get together with a "mama's boy". Anything and everything the MIL says and does, he will believe with no question and no evidence. Please run in the opposite direction the first moment you notice anything strange. You do not want to deal with a "Yes, Mom" all of the time. "I want to go shopping. Can you come with me?" "Yes, Mom. Where do you want to go and what time should I pick you up?" "I want to go out for dinner. Come and join me." "Yes, Mom. Which restaurant are we eating at and what time?" "I'm planning a cruise trip in a couple of months. Would you like to come with me?" "Yes, Mom. I can plan my work schedule around that. Let me know the dates and we can take it from there." "I think her so-called late shifts are her cheating on you. You should set up some hidden cameras." "Yes, Mom. I will go to a spy shop and set it up in the house." And there is that infamous "I don't think those are your kids. You should question her." "Yes, Mom. I will go and get a paternity test." And so on and so forth. While this is not as common, it is a habit that really needs to be broken before they stay single for the rest of his life. Also, this leaves the partner bored and alone, in which makes them get out of the relationship altogether. Save your sanity. With the MIL, by keeping him occupied with his mother, is to try to keep her "baby" close to home.

For couples who have a SAH (stay-at-home) wife and a husband who goes out to work every day, you must watch out for the visiting MIL. She will come visit, or really invade, the home to check on how you clean the home. The timing is sometimes about an hour after the husband leaves for work. Up until he is about to come home from work or even after you serve dinner. The only thing she will do is watch how you do things, and occasionally direct you on how to clean properly (really?). You will have to keep an eye out for her because she will start playing "find the hidden treasure". Yes, she will want to "borrow" something of yours and you will most likely not see it again. Make sure to hide your valuables in a fool-proof safe or a safety deposit box.

Now, this is especially for people of wealth. If you have money from growing up into it, or inheritance, or even the lottery all of a sudden, keep it very well hidden. Live frugally the best you can to not show that you have money. Why do you ask? Once your significant other knows about it, he or she will immediately report it to his or her mother, and she will be sucking up to you. Also, asking for loans and paying their overdue bills. The next thing you know, you will get requested to buy the MIL a car or a trip out of town, even to either remodel their house or buy a brand-new house, WTF!!! And then loan after loan and loan, etc. You will have to stop that dead in its tracks, way before it even starts. Remember: power, money, prestige. The more money and power you have and obtain, the more big-headed the MIL will get. The biggest reason is she would start boasting and bragging that "my DIL is part of a wealthy family" or "my DIL just won the lottery", or something to that nature. She will blow everything so out of proportion. Her friends would want to be around her all the time to possibly leech off DIL as well. The best way to avoid her and the chaos that follows is to keep your distance from her and keep communications only through your husband. No phone calls, emails, or messages.

Epilogue

I always wanted to know what makes the mothers-in-law act the way they do. Hormone imbalance? Menopause? Midlife crisis? My assumption is when they reach a certain age, they had expected to have a certain lifestyle by then. A few things that come to mind are:

A happy marriage: being on the same page of life and responsibilities to get through toward the future.

Two to four children: wanting a big family herself so she can see them grow up to be accomplished children and grandchildren.

Wealth: inherited, earned, or is earning enough to sustain their way of living for her and the family future (mainly for hers, lol)

A nice-sized home: preferrably within a gated community, at least a three to four bedroom, two to three bathroom home to live comfortably in. More than likely with an HOA, lol.

Prestige: being showy, going to parties and galas, and giving donations to charities to always be in with the in-crowd. As well as showing off her (designer) dress and (expensive) jewelry.

Any mother/mother-in-law would love to have all these items in their perfect world. But, with these choices, the "entitlement" or "Karen" comes out and she will start feeling like a "Queen", and start ordering people to do things for her. "You must go here to pick up this", "You have to take me to this place", "You must go there to get that". Who do you think I am? A peasant? A servant? A minion?

Her own "entitlement" will drive anyone and everyone away in a heartbeat. She will always believe her way is the right way, no matter what. And with her driving people away, including family, she will be that crazy cat lady the neighbors are always talking about. Keeping your distance and living your life is the best medicine to cure of MILitis, lol.

www.ingramcontent.com/pod-product-compliance
Lightning Source LLC
Chambersburg PA
CBHW051338150726
47997CB00004B/1515